Disney's

POCAHONTAS

Hippo

Scholastic Children's Books
Commonwealth House, 1–19 New Oxford Street,
London WC1A 1NU, UK
a division of Scholastic Ltd
London ~ New York ~ Toronto ~ Sydney ~ Auckland

First published in the UK by Scholastic Ltd, 1997

© 1996 Disney

ISBN 0 590 19336 8

Typeset by TW Typesetting, Midsomer Norton, Avon
Printed in Italy

STRANGE CLOUDS

Pocahontas never chose the easy path. When her friend Nakoma paddled up the river to bring news that her father had returned from the war, Pocahontas leapt from the top of the cliff where she was standing and dived into the waters of the Chicahominy river. She just missed Nakoma's canoe.

"Show off!" shouted Nakoma, as Pocahontas pushed over the canoe and tipped her into the water.

"They are right when they say that

you fly where the wind carries you," spluttered Nakoma. She had a quiet and careful character, and did not understand how the princess could be so fearless.

Pocahontas fished Meeko, her pet

racoon, out of the river.

He had followed her off the cliff, and landed with an untidy splash in the water. Flit, a tiny humming bird, who Meeko had grabbed in panic as he fell, needed to be rescued from the water too.

Nakoma and Pocahontas were brought up together. Nakoma's mother nursed Pocahontas when her mother died, shortly after the little princess was born. The two young women were like sisters, but they were as different as day and night. Nakoma often wondered if Pocahontas felt her father was sorry that he had not had a son. Did she try to make up for being born a girl by doing all that a man could do? Nakoma and everyone in the village knew that to the chief, his daughter was dearer than anything else in the world.

Pocahontas and Nakoma returned to the village in time to see Kekata, the medicine man, painting the chest of Kocoum, a young and brave warrior.

"He is so handsome," said Nakoma, who was impressed by Kocoum.

"Hmm … I especially love his smile!" whispered Pocahontas, looking at his stern expression. He was so young, so handsome, so brave. He was admired by the whole village, but he never smiled. What girl could want him as a husband?

"My father, you have returned at last," exclaimed the princess. She ran to

embrace Chief Powhatan.

Powhatan was a wise and peaceful man. Many years of battle, followed by talks around the fire had finally brought the local tribes together.

The Chief knew that together they were stronger, and that this strength brought peace. But to keep the peace the tribes needed to stay united.

Her father took Pocahontas by the arm, and they walked to his hut.

"We have much to talk about," said Powhatan.

"Father, I have been having a strange dream," said Pocahontas, eager for her father's advice, "I think it is telling me that something is about to happen."

For many moons, night after night, Pocahontas had dreamt of an arrow spinning above her and then, in her dream, the arrow would suddenly stop.

"Something is about to happen," said Powhatan, smiling. "My daughter, my heart soars with joy – brave Kocoum has asked me for your hand."

"But father, he is so serious," gasped Pocahontas.

"He will be an excellent husband," said her father firmly. "He is loyal and strong. You will be safe with him. You are the daughter of a Chief ... you must take your place among our people." Pocahontas was speechless. She was destined to marry a warrior who did not smile. She listened quietly as her father

told the story of the rushing mountain stream which must, one day, join the calm, steady river.

But she knew she could guide a canoe and follow tracks in the forest as well as any warrior. She was not ready to be calm or steady.

"It was your mother's wish that you would wear her necklace on your wedding day," Chief Powhatan said, as he fastened it around her neck.

She stroked the turquoise necklace.

When she was a child, she had asked if she could try the necklace on, but her father had shaken his head. The necklace was worn to show that a girl was to be married. Playing with it and trying it on for fun was forbidden. Pocahontas wished her mother was alive. But the beautiful wife of Chief Powhatan was not there to give her daughter advice.

But there was someone who could give her advice. In the Enchanted Glade, in a willow tree, there lived a wise old spirit. The spirit was four hundred years old and she knew the secrets of all the women of the tribe. Sooner or later, they all went to her to ask for advice.

Pocahontas jumped into her canoe. She paddled away swiftly and soon left the village far behind.

"My father wants me to be as calm and steady as the river, but the river is not always calm," she thought to herself.

She paddled upstream towards the Enchanted Glade with Meeko beside her and Flit darting along at her shoulder. At a fork in the river she stopped.

"Should I choose the smoothest course, steady as the beating drum? No, I can't!" she cried.

She paddled quickly away from the smooth, wide fork of the river and guided the canoe through the rocks and white water of the other fork. "I must find out what my dream means ... but I fear that Kocoum has nothing to do with it."

She knew she could not spend the rest of her days with a man who never smiled.

The bark of the willow tree came to life as Pocahontas drew near.

A beautiful, old face appeared in the rough bark. Then a warm, husky voice echoed through the Enchanted Glade.

"What a splendid surprise," exclaimed Grandmother Willow. "And you are wearing your mother's necklace."

"That is why I have come to speak to you," replied Pocahontas. "My father wants me to marry Kocoum."

"Kocoum? But he is so serious!" said the spirit thoughtfully.

"That is

what I said! I feel so confused. There is also my dream..." murmured Pocahontas and she told the spirit what she had seen.

"How strange, how very strange," said Grandmother Willow. "It seems to me that this arrow which spins, wants to show you a path – the path that you must follow. Look for your path."

"Grandmother Willow," said Pocahontas anxiously, "how will I know which is the right path?"

"You must listen with your heart..."

Pocahontas was confused. Grandmother Willow's advice seemed as puzzling as her dream.

"Don't you feel that the wind is trying to tell you something? My child, you must be guided by the spirits. The spirits are all around you, in the sky and in the water. Listen with your heart, and they will show you the answer."

Pocahontas took a deep breath. If she

concentrated, she might hear her mother's voice among the spirits of nature.

"Oh, spirits of nature, help me to understand," cried Pocahontas.

She stood up and opened her arms wide in a gesture of offering. Pocahontas listened to the wind. She realised that she

had heard that voice before – she had heard it many times from the top of the cliff above the river, but she had never understood it before. Suddenly she gasped, "You are right, Grandmother Willow. I can hear it! It says that something is coming. I must climb up high."

Pocahontas climbed to the top of the willow and what she saw, took her breath away... against the blue sky she saw strange clouds. They were big and white and not like anything she had seen before. Not even wise Grandmother Willow knew that they were not clouds at all. They were the billowing sails of a ship from a far-away place called England.

LISTEN WITH YOUR HEART

Pocahontas raced through the forest
and then crept slowly through the
bushes and trees near the shore.

"That stranger's hair is the colour of
corn..." murmured Pocahontas. She
could not take her eyes off the pale-faced
stranger. He led the others ashore from
the giant canoe, which was moved by the
strange white clouds.

Meeko, as curious as any racoon,
moved closer to see the strange creature
with eyes as blue as the sky. His sharp

sense of smell told him that the stranger
had food in the sack over his shoulder and
Meeko ran out through the bushes. The
stranger looked startled and pulled a
knife from his belt.

"Meeko, come back," hissed
Pocahontas. But it was too late, the
racoon scampered between the legs of the
stranger.

The pale-faced man was shocked by
the odd creature, but then he smiled and
put his knife away. "And who are you?"
he asked. He
watched Meeko
carefully,
then offered
him a
handful of
biscuits.
She
saw that
Meeko

wasn't in danger, but Pocahontas could feel her heart in her throat. She had an odd feeling that the stranger was something to do with her dream. When the stranger came close to the bushes where Pocahontas was hiding, Flit buzzed out fiercely. He flew at the stranger and threatened him with his long sharp beak. The stranger turned and went back to the beach.

Pocahontas longed to find out more, but she was brave, not foolhardy. She was a Princess, the daughter of a Chief, and her first duty was to return to the village to find out if they knew about the arrival of the strangers. Pocahontas raced along the paths which she knew so well, and soon reached the first huts of the village.

"Have you heard the news, Pocahontas?" Nakoma asked in dismay. "Pale-faced giants have arrived. You must be more careful. Now is not the time to be wandering off alone. Stay in the village!"

Pocahontas was longing to tell Nakoma what she had seen. If Nakoma had been different, they could have had a lot of fun together. Sometimes, this girl, who was like a sister to her, seemed old before her time. Grandmother Willow had four hundred years of wisdom, but she showed more curiosity and daring than Nakoma.

Nakoma was like all the other girls in the village. She was skilled at growing and harvesting maize and she decorated pots beautifully. She cooked well and could cure animal skins. She danced happily at festivals with the other unmarried women. When Nakoma thought of her future, she imagined herself with a man – a good husband. He would be quite handsome, quite kind, quite strong and quite affectionate. He would be a good father to their sons and daughters. Nakoma was a good girl, with a generous heart, but she took no risks and always chose the safest path.

Powhatan and the village elders sent out special patrols to watch the unwelcome visitors.

Pocahontas decided to keep an eye on the stranger who had been kind to Meeko.

She stopped for a moment to wonder if she should tell her father what had happened.

22

But no, Powhatan would worry and scold her, and forbid her to go into the forest alone. He would never allow her to spy on a stranger with hair the colour of corn.

She was as agile as a wildcat and knew every tree, path and stream in the forest. It was easy for her to follow the stranger without him noticing.

"I will stay just behind him, Meeko," she whispered to her friend, as they set off into the forest. "I have to find out what they are doing here. I must find out if it is part of my dream…" She stopped for a moment, and then smiled, "I have to find out why I find him so fascinating."

Flit darted and buzzed around her head even more energetically than usual. He did not think she should be alone in the forest.

Pocahontas was sure she would not be

seen and became careless. John Smith soon knew that he was being watched. She was just above him in the trees when he stopped to drink from the river. She did not realise he could see her reflection in the water. One moment was enough for him to disappear from sight. Where had he gone? Pocahontas felt her heart thump as she searched the pool. He had slipped into a cave behind the waterfall. He waited and stepped out from the curtain of water before Pocahontas had time to run. She looked curiously at his musket, which to her looked like a strange kind of club. She looked at him closely. He was as tall as the tallest warrior, and he stared straight at her with his bright, blue eyes.

She saw his expression change many times. She let her eyes move slowly

over his golden hair, his blue eyes, his pale, pale skin. First, he frowned slightly and put down his musket, but he carried on looking at her.

There was surprise, but there was also something else – something that Pocahontas had started to see on the faces of the men of her tribe, now that she was no longer a child. The Powhatan people respected their Princess, but Nakoma had once laughed and asked her if she had noticed how the young men in the tribe looked at her. Pocahontas had never given it any thought before her friend pointed it out. Since then, she had learned to recognise admiration in the eyes of those who watched her pass by.

Neither Pocahontas nor the stranger looked away. It was as though neither one was willing to lose sight of the other. All of a sudden, the princess realised where she was. She was alone, far from her village and a few short steps away from a stranger. What if he kidnapped her and demanded a ransom from the tribe? She would never forgive herself! Her father would die with worry and shame. She whirled around and darted back to her canoe.

But the stranger called out to her and his voice did not sound dangerous. It was pleading. Maybe he was begging her to stay... Pocahontas knew a couple of words from the languages of neighbouring tribes, but these sounds were different. They meant no more to her than music, or the sound of the wind. Her eyes grew wide as she remembered the words of Grandmother Willow. If she understood the voice of the wind, maybe she could understand the words of this stranger. She suddenly realised that if the stranger with golden hair was a part of her dream, then the spirits could help them to understand each other.

She lifted her head high and waited for him to catch up with her. She would not run away.

"Pocahontas," she said, pointing to herself, "My name is Pocahontas."

Would he understand her? She was clever enough to realise that if his clothes, especially his head-dress seemed odd to her, then to this pale-faced man her dark skin, black eyes and waist-length dark hair must also seem strange.

The stranger replied and his voice no longer sounded like strange music.

"My name is John Smith," he said pointing to himself. She saw the smile on

his lips reach his eyes. He held out his hand to help her from the canoe. When the small dark hand and the large pale hand touched, Pocahontas felt no fear.

SAVAGES

Pocahontas was learning to understand John Smith. "This is a
helmet," he said, taking off the
heavy metal head-dress he was wearing.

"Helmet," repeated the princess,
savouring the sound of the new word.

In her tribe a head-dress was an
important symbol of power. Only the
chiefs, the elders and the medicine men
had the authority to wear one. The
common people were allowed to cover
their heads only for important occasions

such as festivals or weddings.

"Tell me, John Smith, are you a chief among your people?" asked the princess.

"They call me a Captain," admitted Smith, looking embarrassed. He did not know how to explain why the strangers had come from far away to reach her land. How could he tell her that he was a soldier, paid to discover new lands. He travelled the world looking for adventure and wealth. He was responsible for the safety of the expedition, and he would lead his men into battle – against Pocahontas's people, if necessary.

"Tell me, what river is this?" he asked to change the subject. He felt uncomfortable when he saw admiration in her eyes. It made him feel guilty.

"Qui-yough-co-han-nock," said Pocahontas carefully.

"You have very strange names here!"

exclaimed John Smith.

Pocahontas frowned, "Your name is also strange. What does it mean?"

"Well ... nothing really," he replied.

"For my people every name has a meaning ... to me your people are also strange."

John Smith realised that he had said something wrong. He had forgotten that he was having a conversation in his own language with a person who was speaking a very different one, and they understood each other perfectly. He knew that he was not in danger, but there was anger in the Indian girl's voice.

Meeko was hungry so he decided to taste the captain's compass. It looked like a strange biscuit. "Is this bottomless pit your friend?" John Smith asked, changing the subject again. He held out his hand to the racoon. The animal jumped back frightened and almost dropped his precious biscuit.

"Hey, it's only a handshake between friends. Here let me show you, it's our way of saying hello..." he shook Pocahontas by the hand.

At first she seemed as puzzled as Meeko. Flit's wings whirred above Pocahontas's shoulder and he flew angrily at John Smith.

"Flit doesn't like strangers," she said laughing.

The princess lifted up her hand with her palm out and said, "Wing-gap-o," then turned it around in a full circle. "This is how we say hello. And we say goodbye like this," and she turned her hand the other way.

While they talked, Meeko tried to

"We will build streets ... and decent houses," he blundered on, blind to the horrified look on her face.

"Our houses are fine as they are!" said Pocahontas, indignantly.

"It's only that you don't know any better..." continued John Smith. He was disappointed by her reaction, but he was sure he was right, "We have improved the lives of savages all over the world."

The spell was broken. The princess stood up. "Savages are we?"

"I only meant ... uncivilised," he spluttered.

"What you mean to say is ... people who aren't like you," snapped Pocahontas angrily.

John Smith was speechless. Pocahontas stood proudly in front of him. She was a proud princess. But she hesitated ... she wanted him to understand why she was angry. She had to make him see that he was wrong.

She took him by the hand and led him through the forest. If she could not make him understand, then the spirits of nature would help her.

"Everything has a name and a spirit - we are all part of the Earth," she explained gently. "Life is like a huge circle with no beginning or end.

Your people do not understand nature. They see it as something to be used and changed."

A light of understanding shone in John Smith's eyes. Pocahontas felt her heart swell with hope. He was beginning to understand. Her hold on his hand tightened and they began to smile again.

That hot afternoon, John Smith felt his heart beat to a different rhythm. He looked deeply into the eyes of someone he thought was a savage and he learned to understand the voice of the wind.

Pocahontas and John Smith would never forget their wonderful afternoon.

But it was getting late and they soon had to part. Pocahontas felt more and more unhappy and confused.

"How can I like this man, who has shown that he does not understand my people? Who knows if he will ask to see me again…"

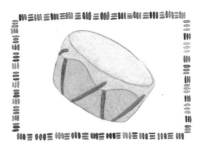

WAR DRUMS

The far-away beating of drums brought her back to reality with a bump. Pocahontas knew what the drums meant – her people were in danger and her place was in the village.

"I have to go," she said jumping to her feet.

"When can I see you again?" John Smith asked, pulling her back.

She had to hurry, she had to run as fast as the wind, but she knew she would do anything to see the pale-faced stranger again.

"I must go now," she said desperately, and wrenching her hand away, she raced into the forest.

"My daughter, the situation is grave," explained Chief Powhatan frowning, when Pocahontas arrived back in the

village. "The pale-faced strangers have cut down trees in the forest to build a barricade around their camp. They have dug enormous holes everywhere. One of them has wounded Namontack, one of my bravest warriors, with a weapon which spits fire."

Not even Kekata's medicines could treat that strange, frightening wound.

"I have no choice ... we will fight these strangers, but we cannot do it alone. We will call on our brothers to help us chase the invaders from our land."

Pocahontas felt her heart sink. The white men had cut down trees and injured Namontack. Was this their way of helping them? Of improving their lives as John Smith had said. She hoped with all her heart that her father could not read her mind. She hoped that Namontack would recover, but above all ... she hoped that she would see the yellow-haired man again.

All the villagers had been told to stay in the compound, but the fields which surrounded them needed to be tended and harvest-time was drawing near.

The next day, while she was gathering corn with Nakoma, Pocahontas saw Powhatan coming across the field. He looked tired and worried.

Pocahontas knew her father wanted her to stay in the safety of their home. But if the other women of the village worked in the fields to make sure there was food for the warriors, the Chief could not forbid her from helping them.

"We are harvesting food for the warriors who are arriving," explained Nakoma.

The princess looked sad and her father thought he knew why. She was worried about her people and she felt like a prisoner in the village. Until the strangers left she would have to live like

a beautiful bird locked in a cage. She could not run through the forest and leap from rock to rock. She could not guide her canoe down the white-water of the river. Powhatan smiled at his daughter.

"When I look at you with the necklace on, I think of your mother."

"I miss her," murmured Pocahontas, thinking that now more than ever she needed her mother's advice.

"But she is still with us," said Powhatan. "Whenever the wind blows through the trees, I feel she is here."

The Chief and Pocahontas smiled

gently at each other.

"I will send Kocoum," said Powhatan as he left them. He knew he could not tell his daughter to return to the village, but he did not like the two girls to be alone in the cornfields. He would be happier if Kocoum was with them for protection.

Pocahontas watched her father as he walked away and she sighed, a deep sad sigh.

"Look!" shrieked Nakoma suddenly. "It is one of them! I will call..."

Pocahontas looked up and saw John Smith coming towards them. She quickly clapped a hand over Nakoma's mouth.

"What are you doing here?" hissed Pocahontas, as Nakoma struggled to make herself free.

"I had to see you again. Yesterday we did not say goodbye."

"Pocahontas ... where are you?" Kocoum's voice became louder as

 he came closer and closer to the two young women.

Pocahontas knew that her father had hurried back to the village and ordered his best warrior to go and look after the princess and her friend. Kocoum had come quickly to protect his promised bride. Pocahontas felt sure that Nakoma would start to scream at any moment and give them away.

She squeezed her friend's hand firmly, hoping that Nakoma would understand.

"I beg you, Nakoma, say nothing!" then she turned to John Smith. "And you, follow me!"

THE COLOUR OF GOLD

"Where are you taking me?" asked John Smith, trying to brush the angry humming bird away. Flit was not happy to see his princess walking away from the village with a stranger.

They crept through the corn

field and into the forest just in time to avoid Kocoum. Then they paddled up the river in a canoe until they reached the Enchanted Glade.

"What a marvellous place," exclaimed John Smith. He was learning quickly. He listened to the voice of the river and the different calls of the animals. He looked in wonder at the soft colours of that peaceful place. "To think that we came all this way to search for gold!"

"What is gold?" asked Pocahontas.

"You know, it is yellow, and it comes out of the ground…" said John Smith waving his arms as he tried to describe it, "…and it's very precious."

"Here take this. We have a lot of that," Pocahontas handed him a cob of corn she had gathered with Nakoma. She was glad to give him something so important.

But John Smith shook his head, "No, gold is … this," he said taking a gold coin out of his pocket.

"Oh, there is nothing like that around here," said Pocahontas.

"All that way for nothing..." the captain murmured. "Well, those boys are in for a big surprise..."

"So you will go home then?" she asked.

"Well ... it's not really home for me. I've never stayed in one place for very long," said John Smith.

"You could stay here," she said, and the words were out of her mouth before she had a chance to think. Then she was ashamed, this was not the behaviour of a Powhatan princess.

The voice of the wind became stronger, and Pocahontas realised that Grandmother Willow was coming to help her.

John Smith jumped to his feet, amazed

and frightened, "What was that?"

"Look," she said, pointing to the willow tree.

"Hello John Smith," said Grandmother Willow, as her smiling face appeared. "Do not be afraid." The spirit studied the Captain's face carefully, "He is kind … and he is very handsome."

Pocahontas smiled when she saw John Smith relax. So, even pale-faced warriors liked compliments. John Smith still looked strange to Pocahontas. Not like a Powhatan warrior at all. She was amazed by his pale skin, his hair and his eyes.

Suddenly a loud voice echoed through the forest.

"Smith! Smith! Where are you, mate?"

The smile disappeared from John Smith's face when he recognised the voices of his friends, Ben and Lon. The Governor must have sent them to look for him. "I'd better go, before everyone comes looking," he said.

"Where can I see you again?"

"Let's meet here ... right here, to-night." And with these words John Smith ran off into the forest.

Sitting at the foot of the willow tree, Pocahontas felt lost and lonely. "What am I doing? I should never see him again..."

"Perhaps, he is your dream," suggested the spirit.

Pocahontas felt hope in her heart, but she was torn between loyalty to her tribe and love for the stranger. "Do you think the spinning arrow was pointing to him?" she asked. Grandmother Willow smiled.

WORDS OF PEACE

Pocahontas raced back to the village. The warriors from the neighbouring tribes had arrived. Pocahontas felt torn in two – if her people and the pale-faced strangers were enemies – her love for John Smith would have no future. She felt a hand caress her shoulder, it was Kocoum. He would never have made such an affectionate gesture before, but now her necklace was a silent promise that she would be his.

"Look at them all," he said. "Now we

53

have enough warriors to destroy the white demons."

Pocahontas frowned. It was no use speaking to Kocoum. But maybe her father would help. She went to meet him, as he strode across the compound towards the hut where the elders were meeting.

"I must speak to you," said Pocahontas anxiously.

"Not now, my daughter," said Powhatan gently, "The elders are waiting."

Pocahontas would not give up so easily. "We don't have to fight them, there must be a better way... we must try to talk to them."

"They do not wish to talk," said Powhatan with a frown.

"But ... if one of them did want to talk ... would you listen to him?"

Pocahontas was blocking the path of her father, the Chief. For a moment Powhatan wondered if he had let his

daughter go too far. But her intentions were good. He knew her heart was full of worry about the war, so he let it pass. "Pocahontas…"

"You would listen, wouldn't you?" she pleaded.

"Of course I would," said the Chief firmly, "but it is not that simple."

Pocahontas watched him take her hand from his arm, and walk sadly away. Pocahontas knew what she must do. She knew that John Smith could convince her people that the white men were willing to talk. As she slipped out of the village, in the dark of night, she heard the voice of her friend, Nakoma. "Pocahontas, do not go out there! I have lied for you once … do not ask me to do it again."

Pocahontas knew that Nakoma had lied to Kocoum. She had not said anything, even though she knew her friend was with their enemy.

To Nakoma, the captain was a stranger. He was one of the men who were destroying the trees, digging giant holes on the shore, and who had wounded her cousin Namontack.

"He is our enemy," said her friend, desperately. "If you go, you will be turning your back on your own people."

Pocahontas could not believe that Nakoma thought that she would forget who she was — the daughter of Chief

Powhatan? Did Nakoma really think she would ever betray her people?

"You are my best friend," insisted Nakoma. "And you are in danger…"

Pocahontas brushed Nakoma's hand away. There was no time to explain. Nakoma would have to trust her.

"I know what I am doing," said Pocahontas, turning to go.

"Pocahontas, no!" gasped Nakoma.

But the princess raced away. She felt certain that John Smith would convince her people. Grandmother Willow would help her find the right words.

The old spirit was waiting for her. "What has happened, my child?"

"The warriors are here…" she had no time to explain because John Smith appeared beside her.

"Pocahontas, listen carefully," he said holding her hands in his, "My men are planning to attack your people, you must tell them straight away."

Pocahontas looked worried. The men in the English camp must be as angry as the warriors in her village.

"You must come with me and speak to my father," said Pocahontas.

John Smith looked worried too. "Talking won't help. I have tried to talk to my men, but everything about this land frightens them."

One of Grandmother Willow's

branches swept the calm surface of the water. Ripples swirled out and washed against the blue-green bank of the river. The spirit spoke gently,

"They are small at first these rings … but look how large they can grow. Someone must find the right path before it is too late," said Grandmother Willow. "At times the right path is not the easiest to follow. Only when there is peace will you be able to stay together."

Pocahontas understood that the wise old spirit was trying to give John Smith the courage to do the right thing.

"Come on, let's go and talk to your father," he said firmly.

He took her in his arms. Her lips touched his. He was going to do this for her, just for her. For the first time, Pocahontas could see how important she was to this man. She was a foreign princess, but he was willing to risk everything to go to her village and speak to her father. Pocahontas knew that no one

would harm him. To the Powhatan, someone who came in peace, from an enemy tribe, was sacred. But John Smith did not know that ... he was very brave.

Suddenly, a piercing war cry made them both jump. Kocoum had seen her kiss John Smith! Nakoma must have told him that she had left the village.

The warrior sprang from the bushes where he was hiding and rushed at John Smith.

"Kocoum! No!" screamed Pocahontas.

A shot echoed though the glade. But who had fired? John Smith did not have his musket with him. He was as shocked as she was. Kocoum had been hit.

A Night Without End

"Thomas!" yelled John Smith. Pocahontas saw the young man. He looked terrified and he was holding the white man's strange weapon. He was the one that fired the shot. He had followed John Smith when he saw him leave the camp. He had only meant to save his friend's life, but Kocoum groaned as he clutched his chest. He grabbed the necklace which Pocahontas wore around her neck. She looked into Kocoum's face. It was full of anger and sadness. Kocoum grabbed the necklace and Pocahontas pulled away. The necklace snapped. It fell in pieces around Kocoum as he fell into the water with a splash.

A strange wound had opened up on Kocoum's chest like a red flower. Pocahontas saw him stop breathing. He died trying to protect her.

"You have killed him!" she screamed. War cries echoed through the forest. They

came nearer and nearer.

John Smith was the first to come to his senses. "Get out of here!" he yelled to

Thomas, who stood frozen to the spot. "Go!"

Pocahontas watched him disappear into the darkness.

The first warriors appeared in the glade. They seized John Smith who had not moved. He did not resist them.

The warriors gathered around the body of Kocoum in the moonlight. They lifted his body carefully and carried it back to the village.

"Who did this?" asked Chief Powhatan.

In his voice, Pocahontas heard the anger and sadness of a man who has lost a son.

"Pocahontas was in the woods. Kocoum went to find her," said a warrior, as John Smith was forced to his knees in front of the Chief, "this white man attacked him."

"Your weapons are strong," roared Powhatan, "but now our anger is stronger. At sunrise, you will be the first to die."

Pocahontas stared at her father in horror. Was this wise, kind Powhatan – this man who spoke angry words of revenge?

"But, father…" she gasped.

"I told you not to leave the village," snapped Powhatan. "You disobeyed me. You have shamed your father."

Pocahontas could not speak. The warriors stared at her, the whole village was watching. Kocoum's lifeless body lay on the grass.

"I was trying to help," she began.

"Kocoum is dead because of your foolishness," shouted Powhatan.

Pocahontas felt her heart thump. There was nothing she could say. Kocoum had died because of her, that was the truth.

She sank to her knees as John Smith was dragged away.

She looked up at Nakoma, "Kocoum was trying to protect me."

"I sent Kocoum to look for you. I was worried and I thought I was doing the right thing," said Nakoma falling to her knees beside her friend.

"It is all my fault," said Pocahontas sadly. She had lost everything, including the respect and trust of her father.

She had caused the death of a man who loved her. And now she was going to lose the man she loved. "I will never see John Smith again."

Nakoma shook her head. If only she had known that the white man would not harm Pocahontas.

"I asked him to come to the village to speak to the Elders," said the Princess. "He was going to do it too. He didn't want war, but now Kocoum has been killed, revenge will be all they want."

"You must see him again," said Nakoma, taking Pocahontas by the hand.

Those condemned to die were kept in a guarded hut. No one was permitted to go there. The princess could ask nothing of her father, because he was angry and no longer trusted her.

"Pocahontas, maybe there is a way," whispered Nakoma. "One of the guards is

Hakatan. You know he likes me. Say nothing, it is worth a try."

Nakoma pulled her through the village.

The guards, armed with spears, stood at the entrance to the hut. Nakoma turned to Hakatan and said the words that the Princess knew at once were the right ones.

"Pocahontas wishes to look into the eyes of the man who has killed Kocoum."

Hakatan hesitated for a moment, frowning. Then with a quick look at the other guard he said, "Be quick," and moved aside to let the Princess go in.

The hut was dark, and John Smith was sitting on the ground. His arms were tied tightly behind his back.

"Pocahontas," he cried, his face lighting up when he saw her.

She ran up to him. "I am so sorry…" For the first time she let the tears run down her face. "Maybe if we had never met, none of this would have happened."

"Pocahontas, look at me," said John Smith, " I would rather die tomorrow, than live a hundred years without knowing you."

Pocahontas stroked his cheek gently. She could not believe they were going to kill him. He would be executed according to the laws of the tribe. How could she bear to see such a thing?

"Pocahontas!" whispered Nakoma, from the entrance of the hut. The guards were getting impatient. They knew they shouldn't have let Pocahontas go into the hut. Time had run out.

"I cannot leave you," she whispered.

"You will never be without me," said John Smith gently. "Whatever happens I will always be with you. For ever."

Pocahontas knew he was trying to stay calm and to give her courage. She knew that crying only made things worse. She

must be calm and courageous too. She
tried to smile, but her lips would not obey.
She had to leave, or she would make
trouble for Nakoma and the two guards.

She moved to the entrance, without taking
her eyes off John Smith. She did not speak
because she did not trust herself not to cry
again, and she could not say goodbye.

THE RIGHT PATH

Pocahontas paddled her canoe quickly through the darkness. She took deep breaths because her heart was beating furiously, and she wanted to be calm. Grandmother Willow was the only one who could help her now. She knew everything.

"They are going to kill him at sunrise, Grandmother Willow," said Pocahontas.

"You must stop them," said the spirit in her warm, husky voice.

"I cannot," said Pocahontas. She had

disgraced herself and her father in front of them all. She had brought shame on her people and she had put them in grave danger.

"My child, you must follow your dream," said the spirit softly.

"I was wrong," said Pocahontas desperately. "I followed the wrong path ... and now I am lost."

Her little friends Meeko and Flit were with her, but now she did not notice them. She sank to the ground, weighed down by guilt and sadness. The little racoon watched her carefully then he climbed up the side of the tree. He reached into his hiding place and took out something shiny.

It was John Smith's compass, shining in the darkness.

Meeko scrambled down the tree again and held it out to Pocahontas. It was the

first time she had seen it properly. She stared at it in amazement.

The dream! The spinning arrow ... here, in this round metal box, was the spinning arrow.

She remembered what John Smith had said about it finding the right path when you are lost.

"The arrow which spins..." she cried.

"It is the same arrow that you saw in your dream," said Grandmother Willow.

"I was right," cried Pocahontas. "The arrow was pointing to him."

The arrow twirled and stopped. It

pointed in the direction of the cliff where the Powhatan executed those who were condemned to death. A beam of light shone on the compass. She realised with a start that it was sunrise.

Her father's words had been clear. At sunrise, John Smith would be the first of the white men to die. He would be executed and his death would signal the beginning of the war.

"It is not too late, my child," Grandmother Willow urged her, "Let the spirits guide you. You know your path, now follow it!"

The tree branches seemed to fall back as she raced through the forest. The wind seemed to hold her up as she leapt from rock to rock. A great energy came from within her. She had to get there in time. As she ran she remembered the night before at the village. The warriors had covered their faces with warpaints.

They chanted as they prepared for battle. They checked their weapons with their agile fingers. They cut and sharpened the arrows, which they would use to kill the white men. It had terrified her. Pocahontas knew that at the English camp, the men had prepared for war too. Their weapons were different, their skin was pale, and their songs had a strange sound. But the thirst for revenge, the desire to fight and to kill, was the same.

The Powhatan warriors wanted revenge for the death of Kocoum.

The white men wanted revenge for the kidnapping of John Smith.

There was hatred in all their hearts. Such hatred could only mean death.

"If he is going to die, I will die too," thought Pocahontas, springing through the forest, as the first light of morning spread through the trees.

The warriors were ready for battle.

They were lined up behind their Chief at the top of the cliff. Below them, the Englishmen loaded their weapons. Would the death of John Smith be their signal to begin the battle? Or would they attack and try to free their captain?

Just as the Chief was about to kill the white man, Pocahontas flung herself on to John Smith's back. She shielded his body with her own.

"No!" screamed Pocahontas. "If you

kill him, you must kill me."

Powhatan hesitated, then his strong voice echoed down the valley, "Daughter, stand back."

"I won't, Father," cried Pocahontas, "I love him." This was the truth. She loved this man with hair the colour of corn, eyes the colour of deep water, pale skin, and warm, gentle voice. A stranger who offered food to Meeko and who knew how to laugh with her. He had learned to understand the voice of the wind. He had bravely accepted death after letting the young man, who had killed Kocoum, run away to safety.

The Powhatan warriors and the white men watched in amazement and curiosity.

"Look around you, look where your hatred has brought us." Pocahontas looked down at John Smith who stared at her in silence. "This is the path which I have chosen, Father. Tell me, which will yours be?"

The wind rustled through the trees, and a wave of brilliant leaves caressed the Chief's shoulder.

Pocahontas watched her father carefully, as he listened to the voice of the wind.

"My daughter speaks with a wisdom beyond her years," he said lowering his

club. "We have anger in our hearts. But she has come here with courage and under- standing. From this day forward, if there is to be further killing..." he looked at John Smith, who waited in silence, "it will not begin with me. Release him."

The warriors freed John Smith. The Englishmen lowered their muskets.

Pocahontas smiled. John Smith took Pocahontas in his arms, then a movement below caught his eye.

Pocahontas followed his gaze. She saw a large man with long, dark hair grab a fire-shooting weapon from one of the white men and point it towards them. He was aiming at her father.

"No!" cried John Smith.

Pocahontas watched John Smith jump in front of Chief Powhatan and push him away.

John Smith's arms dropped to his sides, and he collapsed to the ground next to her. Pocahontas did not scream. She could not make a sound. She had seen it all before, and could not believe that it was happening again. First Kocoum, and now John Smith. He had been shot by one of his own men.

Later, when his wound had been bandaged, John Smith explained what had happened. The large man with dark hair was the Governor, a white man who had been put in charge of the land. He was angry when the Indians laid down their weapons. The Indians were in his way and he wanted their land. The Governor tried to kill the Chief to make sure the battle took place. John Smith's sacrifice had put a stop to this terrible plan. The

men rebelled and the Governor was put in chains and locked up in the giant

canoe with white sails.

Pocahontas was very happy that John Smith was alive, but it took a while for her to understand that he was badly wounded.

"I must return to England. I need to go to a doctor there. The medicine of your people can do nothing for a wound like this."

He smiled as he looked lovingly at her face. Pocahontas understood, by his calm expression, that he felt sure she would go with him. She smiled and kissed his forehead. She told him she had to return to her village before dark.

John Smith nodded. "I will see you

tomorrow. Prepare your things, the ship will sail with the tide."

Pocahontas left the camp. The Englishmen raised their hats to her as she passed them. She was the woman who had saved their captain. She was the one who had stopped the battle. They had seen how greedy and selfish the Governor was and that the Powhatan were peaceful people.

Her canoe was tied up in the usual place, at the bank of the river. Pocahontas climbed in and slowly paddled towards the Enchanted Glade.

Grandmother Willow was expecting her.

"Do you need some more of my bark for young Smith's wound?" the spirit asked.

Pocahontas shook her head. "It is your wisdom that I need, Grandmother Willow. My heart is troubled. I have

reached another fork in the path and I must choose my way. You know that the man I love was injured as he saved my father's life … only in his country can his wound be healed. Grandmother Willow, he wants me to go with him."

"Have you spoken about this?" the spirit asked.

"No, he … is sure that I will go. He says that tomorrow the giant canoe will go away with the tide. He will be waiting for me."

"And what do you want to do?" said the spirit gently.

Pocahontas hid her face in her hands. She was not crying. She was thinking. "I feel older now, Grandmother Willow. It seems a long time since I climbed up your branches and first saw the strange clouds. I feel like a hundred years have passed. I felt sure I would follow the man I love to the ends of the Earth. John Smith comes from a very different land, with very different people. Would they be able to accept me? I do not know, I am not sure." Pocahontas shook her head and sighed. "This is my home and this is the life that I love. John Smith told me that in London people live in big houses. The paths between the houses have no trees. There is a river and maybe sometimes I could go canoeing, but I know that things are very different there."

Grandmother Willow listened in silence.

"My father is not a young man, Grandmother Willow. And now that Kocoum is gone, he will have to find someone to take his place. And then..." She bit her lip.

"What is it?" asked Grandmother Willow softly.

"When John Smith's friends go home they will tell their people what they have seen. Maybe other white men will come here. My people need me ... I understand them. I know what is in their hearts."

The wind blew strongly and whispered something. Pocahontas lifted her head. A sad smile was on her lips.

"Listen to the wind, my child..."

"Grandmother Willow, I already know what it will tell me. I am sure John

Smith loves me. I feel that truth in my heart. He loves me here ... in my land. Would he love me as much in his own city? When he sees me among women with golden hair and pale skin? I do not know ... he is so sure that he knows what I want, that he did not even ask me."

"Will you go to the ship tomorrow?"

The princess stood up. "I know now what I must do."

Nakoma was beside herself with excitement. She rushed around the hut for no reason at all, picking up a bowl and putting it down again, folding a cloth only to unfold it again.

"Oh Pocahontas!" she cried, "If only I could go with you. You will see so many new things."

Pocahontas sat quietly in the corner, cutting Grandmother Willow's bark into small pieces.

Powhatan appeared in the doorway to

the hut, "Daughter! It is time."

Nakoma looked at Pocahontas curiously, "But you haven't prepared your things."

Pocahontas jumped up and smiled "Let's go. John Smith will be waiting for me."

Powhatan held back the curtain which covered the doorway of the hut.

Pocahontas squeezed his arm as she passed him. "Are the baskets of food ready, Father?"

The Chief nodded. He was carrying a cape of richly decorated fur. "Let us go now."

A line of people walked towards the shore. Women carried baskets of food and warriors carried other supplies.

Pocahontas spotted John Smith straight away. He was lying on a stretcher. He was propped up on one elbow, so that he would see her as soon as she arrived.

She walked slowly up to him, carrying the bag of bark she had prepared for him. Powhatan followed a few steps behind her.

"Here," Pocahontas handed the bag to John Smith. "It is Grandmother Willow's bark. It will help relieve the pain."

"What pain?" he asked smiling.

Powhatan gave him the cape. "You will always be welcome among our people. I thank you, my brother."

Pocahontas was kneeling beside John Smith when Meeko jumped up next to them. He was holding something in his paws. "My mother's necklace," said Pocahontas in amazement.

Someone must have picked up the

pieces that were scattered around Kocoum's body. It had been patiently put back together. Pocahontas took the necklace. She looked around wondering who she had to thank. Nakoma smiled at her shyly.

John Smith was looking around for her bags. "Are you coming with me?" he asked, anxiously.

Powhatan looked deeply into his daughter's eyes. "Choose your path," he said, and took a step back, to show he would not interfere.

Pocahontas shook her head and said to John Smith, "I am needed here."

He looked at her for a moment, as if the magic had gone and he did not understand her. "Then I'll stay here with you," he said.

"No, you must go," she said firmly.

"But I cannot leave you," he replied desperately. Pocahontas closed her eyes. She felt like she had in the hut – the hut where he had waited, condemned to die. She repeated the words he had used to comfort her then, "You will never be without me. Whatever happens, I will always be at your side. For ever."

Pocahontas rose slowly to her feet. The tide would not wait and there was nothing more to say.

She ran to the cliff to watch the giant canoe set sail. The wind which filled the ship's sails dried the tears on her cheeks.

Grandmother Willow's bark could not stop her pain. Her wound was one that did not bleed.

She raised her hand in the Powhatan gesture of farewell. She did not know if John Smith could see her, but that did not matter.

"Wing-gap-o," she whispered, moving her hand in a circle. "Until we meet once more."

Eilidh

Eilidh kirkpatrick

Eilidh Kirkpatrick

Eilidh

Eilidh

Jane
Eilidh

EILIDH

KIRKPAT
RICK

On Monday I am getting a new car

I am Looking forward for the weekend